Aussie Bites

Nathan and the ICE ROCKETS

Hardly anyone notices Nathan,
the new boy. Except the school bully.
But when the Ice Rocket competition
begins, people get to know Nathan
for what he really is . . .

which Aussie Bites have **you** read?

Aussie Bites

Nathan and the ICE ROCKETS

Debra Oswald
Illustrated by Matthew Martin

Puffin Books

For Daniel and Joe

Puffin Books
Penguin Books Australia Ltd
487 Maroondah Highway, PO Box 257
Ringwood, Victoria 3134, Australia
Penguin Books Ltd
Harmondsworth, Middlesex, England
Penguin Putnam Inc.
375 Hudson Street, New York, New York 10014, USA
Penguin Books Canada Limited
10 Alcorn Avenue, Toronto, Ontario, Canada, M4V 3B2
Penguin Books (N.Z.) Ltd
Cnr Rosedale and Airborne Roads, Albany, Auckland, New Zealand
Penguin Books (South Africa) (Pty) Ltd
4 Pallinghurst Road, Parktown 2193, South Africa

First published by Penguin Books Australia, 1998

1 3 5 7 9 10 8 6 4 2

Typeset in New Century School Book
by Post Pre-press Group, Brisbane
Made and printed in Australia by Australian Print Group,
Maryborough, Australia

Designed by Debra Billson, Penguin Design Studio
Series designed by Ruth Grüner

National Library of Australia
Cataloguing-in-Publication data:
Oswald, Debra.
Nathan and the ice rockets.
ISBN 0 14 130266 6.
I. Martin, Matthew, 1952– . II. Title. (Series : Aussie bites).
A823.3

One

Let me tell you the story of how I got to know my friend Nathan.

It was just after the October holidays. Our teacher, Ms Zimdahl, stood this kid out the front of the classroom and said, 'This is our new arrival, Nathan Crosby. I hope, Five Z, that you will try to be friendly and make him welcome.'

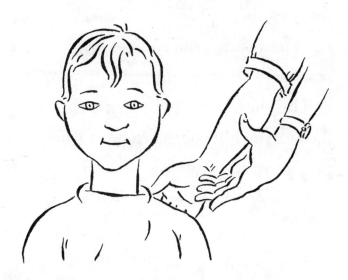

'Yeah. Mmm. Sure. Yes, Ms,' we all mumbled.

Well . . . I have to be honest and tell you that we didn't make much effort at all. Most kids in our class were pretty busy with the friends they already had. Plus, the new kid, Nathan, was incredibly shy and quiet. So quiet that we sort of forgot he was there . . .

Everyone at our school was going wild about the Ice Rockets competition. Ice Rockets are these ice-blocks shaped like spaceships. You can get bright red raspberry ones, bright green lime ones and bright blue – oh, I'm not sure what flavour the blue ones are meant to be. *Blue* flavour, I suppose.

Anyway, when you finished eating an

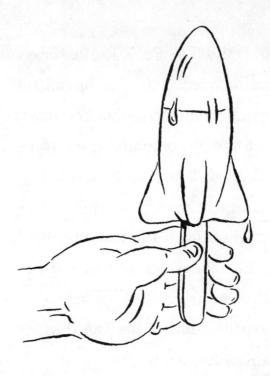

Ice Rocket, you looked on the stick to see if you'd won anything. Lots of kids got a little rocket symbol, which meant they scored a free Ice Rocket. If you collected sticks with a C and D on them, you won a CD player. But by far the best prize was the bike. A limited edition BMX. The BMX Rocket Special. You couldn't *buy* that bike no matter how much money you had. You could only get one by collecting the letters R, O, C, K, E, T and an '!'.

Most lunchtimes I blew my canteen money on an Ice Rocket, even though I don't like them that much. But I would've eaten Ice Rockets for breakfast if it meant getting that brilliant bike.

'You're crazy, Lewis,' said my best friend, Frank Cosentino. 'That competition is a total rip-off.'

'It's not a rip-off,' I protested. 'My cousin's next-door neighbour won some movie tickets and Anna won a free Ice Rocket yesterday.'

'Yeah, yeah, yeah,' said Frank,
waving his hand. (Sometimes Frank
reckons he's the only one who knows
anything, which can be very annoying.)
'They give away lots of *little* prizes,'
he went on, 'so kids like you will get
sucked in and buy *more* crummy Ice
Rockets thinking you can win the bike.
But I bet you can't get all the sticks
in any shops in the whole of
Australia.'

I was beginning to think Frank might be right – until the very next Sunday afternoon. You see, we were hanging around the bike track in our park . . .

Some kids were on Rollerblades and skateboards. Other kids – for example, Frank – rode beaten-up old bikes that still went okay.

I didn't take my bike down to the track any more. It was a present for my seventh birthday and I've 'shot up' since then, my mum says. I look pretty goony on my old bike now. So that afternoon Frank was letting me have turns on his.

That's when a kid from our class called James Dunphy turned up. Turned up at the bike track with – wait for it – a BMX Rocket Special.

Two

You would have to see this bike to really know how brilliant it was. James wheeled it onto the grass in the middle of the track so more kids could get a look at it. The bike frame was shaped as much like a space rocket as it could be and still be a bike. The handlebars, brakes, bell and speedo were all made to look like the control panel of a spaceship. And the body had doodads all over it like something out of *Star Wars*.

When the sun hit that bike, the silver paint was so incredibly shiny that it hurt your eyes. James said it was the

kind of paint they use on real spaceships, and I can believe it.

'How long have you been collecting the sticks?' I asked.

'I got all the sticks in one day,' said James, with this smug grin on his face.

I blurted out more questions. 'How come? Where did you buy the Ice Rockets? What shop?'

'I bought two from the video shop near my auntie's house and my cousin already had an R. I found the rest in the garbage bin at the service station.'

How lucky can you get. Got them all in one day! Found them in a garbage bin! That is so lucky.

Even before he won the BMX Rocket Special, I always thought James

Dunphy was a creepy kid. Always showing off, big-noting himself and making fun of daggy kids. I once saw him bully a little Year-One boy just to impress his dopey friends. In other words, James Dunphy was *not* the kind of person you would say deserved to win a BMX Rocket Special. It just shows you that Ice Rocket competitions don't care if the people who win *deserve* to win. Life isn't always fair.

Of course, now everyone wanted to be James's best friend. Most of the kids at the bike track were sucking up to him and begging for a turn on the Rocket.

Frank and I didn't beg. We decided to hang back and watch. I was so jealous that I could feel my eyeballs just about

bursting out of my head. I was hoping
Frank would say some know-all thing
like 'That bike's not so great'. But he
didn't. He was staring at James's bike
with the same jealous eyes as me.

Then we noticed Nathan Crosby, the new kid. I don't know how long he'd been there. That was the thing about Nathan – he was so quiet, you never realised he'd arrived until he was suddenly there.

Nathan had a bike that was even smaller than mine. A five-year-old's bike. When he rode around the track, he had to stick his knees out sideways to pedal – looking like a frog. Very, very goony.

Nathan made the mistake of riding near to where James was posing and boasting. James couldn't resist the chance to make fun of him. He spluttered into the kind of nasty laugh he does and pointed at Nathan. The other kids were so desperate to suck up to James that they all laughed, too.

'Hey, dogbreath,' sneered James. 'Great bike. Can I have a turn?'

The other kids laughed like that was

the funniest thing they'd ever heard.

Nathan didn't even look around.
He just keep circling the track on his
little bike.

'How come you've got such a cool
helmet and such a pathetic bike?'
yelled James.

It was true that Nathan had a cool helmet. It looked brand new – with sparkly purple swirls all over it, like an astronaut in a science-fiction show would wear.

'Give us your helmet and I'll give you a turn on my Rocket bike,' James smirked.

'No, thanks,' said Nathan and he kept on riding around and around.

Oh boy, now I hated James Dunphy more than ever. I reckon if a person wins a brilliant bike as easily as James did, then that person should take a break from being a nasty bully. Someone as lucky as James Dunphy can afford to be nice to a daggy new kid like Nathan Crosby.

'Should we go and talk to Nathan or something?' I asked Frank.

'Probably, yeah . . . poor guy,' Frank mumbled.

But in the end we didn't move. We couldn't think of what to say. And Nathan was such a shy person, we couldn't be sure he *wanted* us to talk to him.

Still, I tried to smile in his direction,

to let Nathan know we were on his side. But he didn't notice me. His eyes were fixed on James's bike. I could see the shiny silver paint from the BMX Rocket glinting in Nathan Crosby's eyes.

Three

Nathan reckons he still remembers
that afternoon like it's a video he can
play over and over in his head. He
remembers how he rushed straight
home from the bike track and smashed
open his Spiderman moneybox.

He'd been saving up to go halves with
his parents on a new bike. Saving all
his pocket money, the birthday money
from his nanna, plus coins he found in
the street. The fabulous sparkly purple
helmet he wore at the bike track was
a present from his mum and dad as
'an incentive' for him to save.

But Nathan was sick of waiting and

saving. He wanted that BMX Rocket
Special. I guess he thought that if he
had a fantastic bike, then kids would
want to be his friend, the same way
they wanted to be James's friend.
I know, I know . . . kind of a dumb
thing to think. But you must
understand that Nathan Crosby was
a shy, lonely, desperate kid. And he
thought winning the Ice Rocket
competition was the answer to all
his problems.

Nathan had a plan. Every day he
brought some of the moneybox coins to
school to buy six Ice Rockets from the
canteen. He always bought two of each
colour, figuring that might increase his
chances. Then on the way home from

school, he would buy one more from the corner shop.

After lunchtime, Ms Zimdahl kept doing her little worried frown when she looked at Nathan.

'Why is your mouth all blue, Nathan?' she asked. 'And why is your tongue bright green? Are you sick?'

'Ith's justh from eating Ithe
Rockethes, Mith Zthimdahl,' he said.

'Why are you talking like that?
What's wrong with your mouth?' she
wanted to know.

'My lipths and my tongue are
a bit frothzen,' he explained.

'Well, maybe you should go
easy on the Ice Rockets
from now on, Nathan,'
she suggested.

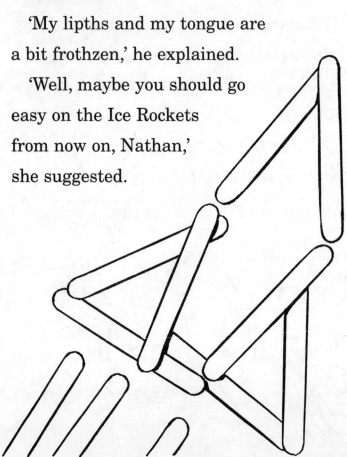

But Nathan couldn't afford to go easy.
By the end of the first two weeks,
he had the R, the O and the T sticks.

Frank and I started to watch Nathan
in the playground at lunchtime,
chomping and sucking his way through
six Ice Rockets.

'You've got to admire his determina-
tion,' I said.

'Oh yeah,' agreed Frank. 'I hope he
wins that bike, y'know.'

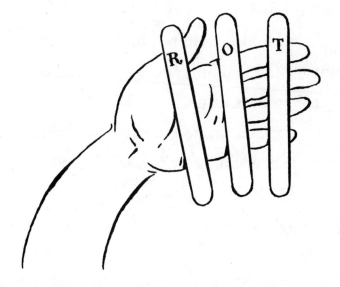

But as the weeks went by, Nathan kept getting more of the same, never a C or a K or an E. And there was no sign of an '!'. Nathan knew that ROT wasn't going to win him the Rocket. The only solution was to trade sticks.

If you think about it, going up to kids he didn't know and asking to trade sticks was a scary thing for a shy person like Nathan Crosby. But he was so determined to win that bike, Nathan had to be brave.

Frank and I could see him across the playground, looking down at his sticks and then over at us.

'Do you reckon he's deciding whether to come over and talk to us?' I asked.

'Yeah, I reckon he is,' said Frank.

I smiled as hard as I could so
the smile would reach across the
playground to Nathan. And over
he came.

'Hi,' we said.

'Hi . . .' mumbled Nathan nervously.
'Are you collecting Ice Rocket sticks too?'

'A few,' I said. 'Wanna swap some?'

'Oh, yeah!' said Nathan, breathing
out with relief.

So we laid our sticks on the ground
to see if we could swap. But it turned
out I had all the same letters as
Nathan anyway.

'Thanks for trying . . .' said Nathan,
starting to walk away.

I felt Frank nudge me in the ribs.
He flicked his head at Nathan as if to
say 'we should talk to him'. So I said,
'So how's your collection going, Nathan?'

And that's how we really got started
talking to Nathan Crosby.

Four

The next lunchtime, Frank and I sat with Nathan to help eat through the six Ice Rockets. We had another good chat with him and found out that Nathan is actually a very interesting person.

He's lived in different countries all over the world, because of his mum's job. (That's why he turned up at our school three-quarters of the way through Year Five).

Nathan's lived in Japan, Italy, Brazil, Kenya and one other place I forget right now. He knows a stack of fascinating facts about those places and he tells some excellent stories. Plus, he has a very good sense of humour and a truly impressive fingernail-clipping collection.

But Nathan was having no luck with the competition sticks.

'Y'know,' said Frank, 'I heard that Mr Kerr has an E stick up on a shelf in the staffroom.'

'Do you reckon he'd swap it with me?' asked Nathan eagerly.

'It's worth a try,' I said.

'Oh, but Mr Kerr . . .' murmured Nathan. Mr Kerr was the Year-Six teacher and he was kind of a scary guy.

'We'll go with you,' offered Frank.

So the three of us marched down to the staffroom to talk to Mr Kerr. On the way I whispered to Frank, 'I thought you thought the Ice Rockets competition was a rip-off.'

'I do,' whispered Frank.

'So why are you doing this?'

'I think the guy deserves a decent chance.'

We knocked on the staffroom door and luckily Ms Zimdahl opened it. When she saw Nathan standing there with Frank and me, her face opened up into a big smile. I think she'd been worried about Nathan looking left out and lonely.

'Is Mr Kerr here?' asked Frank. Frank is by far the bravest out of us kids.

As soon as he heard his name, Mr Kerr tipped back his chair and squinted

through the doorway at us. I jumped
with fright.

'What could The Three Musketeers
want with me?' he hooted. 'Does it take
three of you to talk to me?' (You must
understand that Mr Kerr thinks he's
a very funny guy.)

After Frank gave him a little push, Nathan stammered out his question about the E stick.

Mr Kerr did a big act about how he wasn't sure whether he wanted to give up his E stick. 'I might want a Rocket bike myself,' he said. Ha – as if a bloke like Mr Kerr would want that bike. It turned out he was just teasing Nathan (which is another example of Mr Kerr trying to be funny).

Eventually he got the stick down
from his shelf. I could see Nathan's eyes
flash when he saw the E.

'I can't just *give* you a valuable thing
like this, can I?' said Mr Kerr, dragging
it out to make Nathan suffer.

'Oh . . .' said Nathan, not sure what
he was supposed to say.

Frank jumped in (trying to be helpful) and asked, 'What if he swaps you for it – for one of the other prizes?'

'Mr Cosentino,' Mr Kerr frowned at Frank, pretending to be super-serious, 'what would I want with Ice Rockets and a skateboard? No, no, no, I'm not interested in swapping.'

Nathan slumped down. He started to shrink back towards the door, giving up, when Mr Kerr made a loud sucking noise with his mouth.

'I think you'll have to *earn* this stick. Now what job can I get you to do?'

And that's how Nathan ended up, every lunchtime that week, cleaning the chewing gum off the bottom of the desks in Mr Kerr's classroom. Some of the blobs were still sticky and disgusting, and the dried-out bits took ages to scrape off. But when the job was finished, Mr Kerr kept his word and gave Nathan the E stick. Mr Kerr may be a bit of a nerd but he's not a total creep.

Five

All Nathan needed now was a C, a K and an '!'. But as he ate Ice Rockets day after day, those letters never showed up.

I was heading out the school gate one day when my friend Marion hissed to get my attention.

'I hear you've got a friend who's looking for a C,' she said.

'Have you got one?' I gasped.

'No. But I might know someone who has.'

So that's why I introduced Marion and Nathan the next lunchtime. Marion is almost as shy as Nathan so I don't think they would *ever* have started

talking to each other without the Ice
Rocket problem. But, in fact, they have
a lot in common and got on straight
away.

Marion knew a kid called Eli in Year
Six who had two Cs. Eli was prepared
to swap one of his Cs for a D so that
he could get the CD player.

'Okay, let's go!' said Nathan,
desperate to get another letter.

'Wait a minute,' said Frank.
'You could hang onto your D and
maybe you'll win the CD player. I bet
it's easier to get than the bike.'

I could see Frank's point. 'Yeah,
Nathan,' I said. 'A CD player would be
cool. I mean, a CD player's better than
ending up with nothing.'

Nathan's face scrunched up for a moment as he thought about this. Was he going to give up the chance for the Rocket Special to get a CD player? No! He shook his head and stuck to his guns.

A week after doing the swap with Nathan, Eli brought his new CD player to school. He waved hello to Nathan across the yard and we could see him explaining to all the other Year-Six kids about the trade. After that, lots of Year-Six kids were interested in how Nathan was going. They'd wish him luck, offer him their Ice Rocket sticks and other friendly stuff like that.

All Nathan needed now was a K and an '!'. That bike was so close Nathan could practically feel its wheels spinning under him. He could almost squeeze his hands on those shiny silver handlebars.

Nathan's brain was working overtime. 'Not everyone who eats Ice Rockets cares about the competition,' he told us. 'Lots of people just throw their sticks away. I've got to get hold of those sticks.'

So that's how come Frank, Marion and I met up with Nathan at the corner shop after school. Every time we saw someone buy an Ice Rocket, we'd ask if we could have their stick when they finished. Some grumpy people told us to get lost but most people were pretty friendly about it. One of us would follow them down the street as they ate their Ice Rocket, then grab the stick and run back with it.

Kyet, the bloke who runs the corner shop, didn't know what we were up to at first. But once we explained, he was right behind Nathan. Kyet even slipped him the odd free Ice Rocket to help him along.

We hung around the corner shop using this method for three days in a row. On the fourth day, Nathan said, 'Why are you guys helping me like this?'

'Dunno,' I shrugged. 'It's exciting – like being in a movie or something. Except that it's about Ice Rocket sticks instead of big movie stuff.'

'Plus we think you've got guts,' said Frank.

The next thing we knew, Marion was

making this screeching noise up the street. She came belting back towards us — away from the little kid in a stroller who'd just finished a red Ice Rocket.

'I've got it! I've got it!' yelled Marion.

'Got what?' yelled Nathan.

'An exclamation mark!'

She threw the stick the last couple of metres and it landed straight into Nathan's hand as if that stick *belonged* there. We all looked down at the '!' sitting in his palm. For a minute, we were all too excited to breathe. No one wanted to say too much about the K in case we jinxed it.

Frank was the first to speak. 'We meet here tomorrow – same time, same place.'

Six

When I got home I didn't even tell my mum about the '!'. The week before, she had snapped at me, 'I don't want to hear one more word about that wretched competition, Lewis.' And I didn't blame her. I must have been pretty boring, going on and on about it every day.

But after dinner, when we were watching TV, an ad came on about the Ice Rocket competition. The competition was closing on Friday! No prizes could be claimed after Friday and whatever sticks you had would be worthless. So Nathan's ROC ET! would be worth *nothing*.

I couldn't help squawking at the TV.
Mum thought I was having an attack
or something. I babbled out the whole
story, even though I wasn't supposed to
go on about Ice Rockets any more. Mum
was very sympathetic about it anyway
(she's a nice person, my mum) and said
she felt sorry for Nathan, too.

It took me ages to get to sleep that night. Nathan only had one day left. I could imagine him lying in bed, with his fabulous sparkly purple bike helmet glistening on the bedside table.

The first thing I saw when I arrived at school the next morning was Nathan huddled in a corner with James Dunphy. I was confused at first, until I worked out what was going on. Nathan was selling his sparkly purple bike helmet to James for $25. (Don't ask me where James got the money. That creepy kid always has heaps of money from somewhere.)

James walked away with a snigger – he knew he'd got a great helmet really cheap. But Nathan was desperate –

the moneybox cash was down to $4.80
and there was only one day to go. If he
added his moneybox coins to the money
from James, he had a total of $29.80 to
make a last-minute, all-out go for
the bike.

At lunchtime, Kyet (the bloke from the corner shop) turned up at the school gate with a whole pile of Ice Rockets. There were so many that they were still packed in the cardboard cartons from the shop freezer. After Nathan paid for those, he used the rest of his money to buy out every last Ice Rocket in the school canteen. Forty-nine in total.

Frank and I organised all the kids in Years Five and Six. (I mean all the kids except James Dunphy and his mates — they were too busy laughing at Nathan to help out.) Kids sat lined up along the silver benches near the canteen.

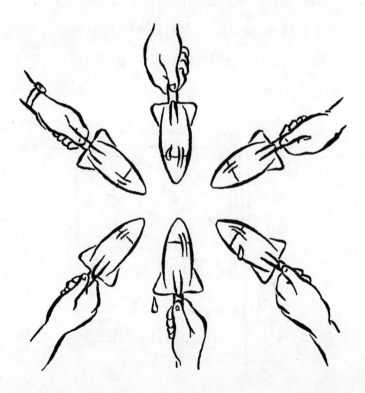

Nathan walked along the rows handing out Ice Rockets, in whatever flavour each person wanted. Every kid understood that the second they finished, they would hand the stick to Nathan.

Finally, Frank and I sat down on the assembly-hall steps and tore the wrappers off ours. Frank's mouth was quickly blue from his Ice Rocket. I'd gone for the lime green. I was so hyped-up my hand was shaking, so I could just imagine how nervous Nathan must have been.

Nathan couldn't keep still. He prowled up and down the rows of silver seats, waiting for the first stick. There was hardly any talking. In fact it was so quiet, all you could hear was the sound of forty-nine kids sucking and slurping on Ice Rockets.

I saw the venetian blinds on the staffroom window flick backwards. The teachers were busting to know what was going to happen, even though teachers have to pretend they're not interested in silly kid stuff like Ice Rocket competitions.

Murray Begg finished his raspberry Ice Rocket before anyone else. (Murray Begg has always been a piggy eater. If you saw him eat a pineapple donut you would know what I mean.)

'Hey, look what I got!' guffawed Murray.

Nathan leapt over to him. It was just a rocket symbol, for a free one.

'You can keep it, Murray,' said Nathan, trying not to sound too disappointed. There were still forty-eight Ice Rockets to go. Forty-eight chances for a K.

One by one, kids held their sticks up in the air to show they'd finished. No sign of a K so far. If people scored a free Ice Rocket or even the movie tickets, Nathan always said they could keep them. Everyone was getting first-hand experience of what a generous kid Nathan was.

'How are you going with yours?' I asked Frank. I was about halfway through mine.

'Look, Lewis,' said Frank, 'I don't want to be a downer or anything . . . but you know the chances of finding a K are pretty low.'

'Forty-nine is a lot of Ice Rockets,' I pointed out.

'Get real. The K is obviously the key to the whole thing. The people who run the competition only let out exactly the right number of Ks. That's how they make sure they don't give away too many Rocket Specials.'

The thing about Frank is that he usually makes a lot of sense. Even when you don't want him to. But there was no way I was going to give up hope.

'Well, James Dunphy must've found a K,' I argued.

'Yeah . . .' growled Frank, scrunching up his lip. (He likes James even less than I do.) 'Don't remind me or I'll throw up blue Ice Rocket all over you.'

Right at that moment, I broke through the last layer of green to reveal the stick. Just a lousy T.

Then Frank said, 'Oh . . .'

'Oh what? What have you got?' I demanded.

'No, I mean O, not "oh". I've just got an O.'

'Oh . . .' I muttered.

We were down to the last few kids.
It wasn't looking good for Nathan and
the Rocket Special. I could hardly bear
it and I reckon most of the kids felt the
same way. It was even more quiet than
before – just a few kids still slurping
and no one even daring to speak.
By now the teachers had lifted the
venetian blinds right up so they could
look out – not bothering to pretend they
weren't interested any more . . .

Seven

Robert Janascewska was the last kid still eating. Only one chance left.

'Hurry up, Robert!' someone yelled. 'Eat faster!'

We were all staring at Robert. Waiting. But Robert was taking his time with his red Ice Rocket, sucking on it slowly. (Robert Janascewska is basically a nice kid but he can be irritating sometimes.)

In a movie, the K would definitely be under the last Ice Rocket. They do that to keep the suspense going for as long as possible and make it more exciting. But this wasn't a movie. This was just

our playground at lunchtime and there
was no K. Just another stupid O.

One enormous groan went through
Years Five and Six. You could tell
that every kid felt bad for Nathan.
Everyone was barracking for him
to win that bike.

I turned around to Nathan. 'Hey
mate, maybe –'

But he had already gone, vanished.

'Where'd he go?' said Frank.

'Dunno,' I said. 'He must be pretty upset.'

Then I caught a glimpse of Nathan's shoes, disappearing round a corner. He was scooting down the street towards the bike track. I was about to head off after him, when the bell went.

Ms Zimdahl frowned, her eyes scanning the classroom. She knew something wasn't right. Everyone (except James Dunphy) was acting so quiet and sulky.

'Where is Nathan Crosby?' she asked.

James let out a nasty hoot of laughter and began, 'Nathan's probably gone –'

Frank's arm shot out and pinched James hard on the elbow.

'Ow!' whined James.

I jumped to my feet. 'Oh, Nathan felt really sick at lunchtime so he walked home to lie down. It's okay, Ms Zimdahl, he's got his own key,' I lied.

We glared at James so fiercely that he didn't dare dob Nathan in.

Ms Zimdahl still seemed worried. 'Well, in future, Nathan shouldn't go off without telling a teacher.'

I was shaking a bit when I sat down. That was the first time I'd ever told a lie to Ms Zimdahl. She's the best teacher I've ever had and I felt lousy fibbing to her. But I guess it was a sign that Nathan Crosby had become a good friend of mine. I mean, I wouldn't lie to my favourite teacher for just *anyone*.

As soon as the last bell went, Frank, Marion and I bolted out the gate and headed for the park.

As we expected, Nathan was at the bike track. He was walking around and around the loop. Every time he got to the spot where he'd first seen James Dunphy's Rocket Special, he'd stop and stare. I bet Nathan could still imagine

the bike sitting there, with its space-
rocket silver paint shining in the sun.

'What can we say to him?'
I whispered.

Frank shrugged. We didn't have
a clue. We just knew that Nathan was
our friend and, at a time like this,
we couldn't leave him on his own.

So we started walking around the
bike track beside him. To begin with,
Nathan didn't say anything, as if it
was perfectly normal for four kids to
go around a bike track, on foot,
not speaking.

On the third loop, Nathan looked up
with a tiny bit of a smile. I suppose he
was grateful that we were there. Boy, if
I'd been through what Nathan had been

through, I'd be crying and moaning and feeling sorry for myself. But Nathan was being so cool about it. What an impressive kid.

On the fourth loop, Frank and I started being silly. We pretended we were really riding bikes, overtaking each other, making the sounds of tyres screeching. Marion started doing

figure-eights on her pretend bike. Frank
kept doing wheelies and bicycle stunts
until he managed to make Nathan laugh.

Then Frank stepped off the bike
track and pretended to pick up another
bike. He wheeled the invisible bike over
to Nathan and offered it to him. 'Race
ya,' whooped Frank and zoomed off.

Eight

A second later, Nathan was running after Frank, pretending to ride his own bike.

The four of us had this loony 'bike' race around the track with our invisible bikes. I know it sounds weird and it must have *looked* weird. But *doing* it was actually a lot of fun.

We got faster and faster until we crashed into each other in a huge stack. We staggered back off the track onto the grass, all panting, too out-of-breath to move.

Then Nathan suddenly burst out laughing.

'What?' I asked.

Nathan shook his head, laughing too much to speak.

'What?' Frank asked.

'My parents can't stop yelling at me and they reckon I've gone mental. And now I've got no bike, no other prizes, no helmet and I spent every cent I'd saved up to buy a bike,' Nathan explained.

I suppose it might sound funny –
if someone told you the story and it
hadn't actually happened to *you*.

Then he laughed again and said,
'I did end up with some friends, though,'
and flopped out flat on his back.

These days Nathan hangs around with
our group most of the time. But he's
pretty popular with lots of kids now.
Considering he's still a very shy person.

You could almost say that Nathan
is famous at our school. Everyone
remembers the Ice Rocket competition –
how Nathan went so over-the-top and
how he gave away lots of prizes. And
how he never whinged or chucked a
wobbly about not winning in the end.

Now, Eli and other Year-Six kids always stop to say hello to Nathan. Mr Kerr usually makes cracks to him about chewing gum. Kyet from the corner shop tries to give him free Ice Rockets, but Nathan can't face eating them any more.

By the way, you might be interested to know what happened a few weeks later. James Dunphy's Rocket Special was wrecked. James told some story about riding his bike really fast on the highway and slamming into a semi-trailer in a spectacular stack. But no one believed James and his big mouth.

Word got around that James really left his bike in the driveway and his mum ran over it when she backed out